This story isn't for those who world as they will not know "vanilla" means or what a collaring ceremony is all about. Okay, you're obviously curious to know the meaning of both, so I shall put you out of your misery.

First "vanilla" as we all know is the most boring of all the flavours of ice cream available. In the kinky world, which I belong to, it's also a collective word for straight non-kinky people. You know those odd, strange people who have sex in the missionary position, there are known in the kinky world as vanilla.

Now to explain what collaring is all about. A collaring ceremony is a symbolic gathering between two or more people and a group of friends to honour a commitment. It is a commitment of a Master or Mistress to their slave and vice versa. It isn't a frivolous occasion and is mostly taken very seriously by those being collared. The ceremony is often compared to a wedding in that it involves vows and a pledge of commitment. Instead of a ring placed on the bride and groom's finger, a collar is placed around the submissive's neck. Just like a wedding ring a collar is usually worn all the time.

A collaring ceremony does not have one male groom and one female bride. It can be a ceremony between any number of people in a relationship with any gender. A collaring ceremony is used by those who are seriously into the BDSM lifestyle. However, it is mostly it is a celebration between a single slave and his or her Master.

Collaring ceremonies are not bound by tradition as most weddings are. Each collaring is unique to the people taking part and can be completely different from those that have gone before it. There are no rules to adhere to. Those planning the ceremonies are free to shape their celebration into whatever they want it to become.

Now you know what collaring is, let's eavesdrop on the lives of a Mistress and her slave who are soon to enter into the serious commitment of a collaring.

Meet Shiela or for the purposes of this story Mistress Anastasia as she prefers to be known by others in the BDSM scene. Mistress Anastasia lives in central London and is a German lady in her mid to late fifties. She is a tall, dark, commanding, and elegant lady who is deeply into the kinky lifestyle. Mistress Anastasia's interest in BDSM began about ten years ago when she met her then-husband. He was a mid to high-ranking serving officer in the

British Army based on the Rhine. Whilst serving in Germany, he met Anastasia who was around fifteen years younger than himself. They married and moved back to London at the end of his service.

They were not long into the relationship when Mistress Anastasia realised her husband was kinky and liked to dominate, whip, and cane women. Mistress Anastasia accommodated his need to dominate and together they went to many fetish clubs in the London area. During these visits, it soon became apparent that Anastasia herself was dominant, which potentially created an incompatibility, as her husband wanted Anastasia to be a compliant slave and didn't like the idea of his wife having dominant desires and needs.

However, in all other respects, the marriage worked well, and to save the relationship

Anastasia and her husband Roger came to a compromise to suit them both.

The solution to their problem was that her husband was allowed to continue to dominate his wife and other women on the proviso Anastasia could have her own slave to dominate and serve her. This was a way to satisfy both their needs and they decided to hold kinky parties at their home at the weekends. Anastasia's husband Roger had a fundamental problem. There were simply not enough single women in the BDSM community to satisfy his needs, especially in his age group, as they were all married. The solution was to invite couples to their parties with the knowledge that the female guest would be dominated by Roger during any session.

This arrangement worked really well. Once a month they would hold a party and they would invite a willing couple along to play. Usually, it ended up with Roger dominating the woman whilst Anastasia played with and dominated her husband.

The kinky parties hadn't escaped the attention of their neighbours and soon there were rumours of orgies and drugs in an otherwise respectable middle-class neighbourhood. Eventually, the couple's antics brought unwanted attention by the police and one evening the house was raided for drugs. No drugs were found on the premises, but unfortunately, Roger has a working revolver, a relic he acquired whilst serving in the Army. It's a shame really as he wasn't by any strength of the imagination a violent man or criminally minded. The revolver was merely a toy, a keepsake, he had not the slightest intention of ever using it.

Nevertheless, the firearm brought loads of unwanted attention as Roger was arrested and not only made the local newspapers but the national ones too because he was a high-ranking army officer with a kinky connection which lead to his arrest. He was eventually dishonourably discharged from the Army. In those days the Army would frown on his proclivities and a criminal conviction was enough to see him cashiered. This puts a strain on the relationship and it broke down. One year later Roger and Anastasia divorced.

For the next few years, Anastasia returned to her vanilla life. Although on the whole, she was quite happy, something was missing in her life and slowly and surely, the need for submissive men returned. Mistress Anastasia's appetite for the kinky lifestyle was rekindled. For quite a while, she satisfied her primal needs by attending some of the many BDSM and fetish clubs in and around London.

Anastasia was also becoming very successful in her career and she longed to own her own submissive who could cook and keep the house clean while she was at work. Someone she could own, manage, mould, and shape to her own needs and requirements. A slave that was hers and hers alone, not a borrowed submissive for an evening session at a club.

Mistress Anastasia began her search at the various Munches held in and around the city. The problem with Munches is although it is an excellent way to have a drink and meet like-minded people locally, it wasn't good for dating, as nearly all attendees were couples and very few single people would come to the Munches on their own.

Mistress Anastasia had an idea on how to find the submissive of her dreams, she decided to advertise for a suitable 24/7 submissive slave to cook and provide domestic service. The advertisement was placed in all the kinky magazines and websites. The idea was to get all the applicants to meet her in a hotel room for an interview.

Anastasia decided on a posh hotel in the centre of London. The idea was to get all applicants to come to the hotel for an interview over a space of a week and then shortlist possible suitable applicants. She needed to set a criterion for her prospective slave. The chosen slave will need to be male, fit, single, and under 50 years of age. He needed to be, not necessarily educated, but of a good standard of intelligence. Anastasia wanted someone she could relate to and converse with during down periods. The suitor needed to be clean, tidy, and well-turned out.

The slave needed to be open-minded and above all supremely submissive. He also had to have a deep-seated natural need to idolize and worship women, in particular his Mistress. Of course, he also had to be able to endure the pain of punishment and accept graciously liberal amounts of humiliation.

Initially, the prospective slave had to email Mistress to give a brief account of himself so Anastasia could deduce whether or not it was worth the time and expense of interviewing him. Anastasia was more than surprised when she was bombarded not with hundreds but thousands of emails. In fact, she had so many replies she couldn't answer them all. In the end, she had to delete many hundreds of emails as she would never have the time to read them.

The sad part was the vast majority of applicants she did select were either timewasters, fakes, or wannabes. At the end of the day, only half of one percent of those who replied were genuine in wanting the position.

More disappointing still only a tiny fraction of those genuine applicants were suitable and when the time came for interviews only five applicants have been invited out with an initial 2000 plus inquiries.

Anastasia made arrangements for the five applicants, to come to the hotel in London for an interview. She had set aside one hour for each applicant, she felt that was enough time to know if they were suitable. On the chosen day Mistress Anastasia arrived at the hotel early. She dressed elegantly in a two-piece cream suit and matching heels. She looked to all who saw her like a highly professional business lady. She decided to meet each applicant in the foyer and ask a few questions to access their suitability before inviting them to her room in privacy for a more in-depth interview.

The day was plagued with disappointment the first three applicants failed to arrive. This annoyed Anastasia very much after all the effort she had put into the venture and the costs involved and three didn't have the decency to show up.

The fourth a Scot was so drunk he could hardly stand up. He was wracked with nerves and thought a pint of beer in a nearby pub would settle him down. One pint turned into many. Anastasia was quick to dispatch this applicant as he reeked of alcohol and was slurring his words badly.

Almost in despair Mistress, Anastasia waited for the final applicant to arrive. After a long impatient wait, Anastasia looks at her watch and realises her last interviewee was ten minutes late for his appointment. Just when she was about to give up a young man walks across the foyer and approached Anastasia.

Chapter Two

Meet Paul.

Sweating profusely a young slim man with a pleasant smile approaches Anastasia. Mistress Anastasia looks up at the boy. At least, that is how Anastasia saw him as just a boy, although he must have been in his early forties. Nevertheless, he had a baby face and a shy boyish charm.

"Come and take a seat beside me." Mistress Anastasia said with a welcoming smile. Once Paul has sat Anastasia's expression changed to one of dismay as her smile dissolved into a frown.

"First, before we chat," Mistress Anastasia said, raising her voice slightly for effect. "This is an interview for an important position as my slave and you arrive ten minutes late, keeping me waiting. I was just about to give up, get up and leave. That is not a good start, is it? " Mistress Anastasia paused to see if her words were having any effect on Paul. Paul seemed to sit there stunned and said nothing so Anastasia continued:

"What's more, to add insult to injury, you come to a prestigious hotel like this one and you're dressed in jeans and a tee shirt. What have you to say for yourself? " She asked, pausing for Paul's answer. Paul stuttered for a bit and blurted out his reply.

"I am sorry Mistress for being late. I didn't have time to change clothes and it's very hot today.

Also, the traffic in the centre of London was much worse than I expected."

"That's no excuse, no excuse at all," Mistress Anastasia barked whilst brushing her long hair from her eyes. "A good slave is never ever late. In future if I take you on, you'll leave home in good time, lateness won't be tolerated. I will let you off on this one occasion because you haven't had any training in obedience.

"Does that mean I have the position? " Paul asked with a flicker of excitement.

"No, it doesn't, and now explain your slovenly appearance. I am surprised they let you into this hotel as they have high standards, and so do I," Mistress Anastasia added.

"The temperatures outside are nearly eighty degrees. It's too hot to wear a suit," Paul replied somewhat feebly.

"I am wearing a suit" replied Mistress Anastasia. "I have taken the trouble to appear smart for you, so why haven't you given me the same courtesy?"

Paul gave up and just looked into his lap whilst he searched for inspiration for something to say to impress. Anastasia sensed his discomfort and decided not to make him squirm any longer.

"We'll move on. I will overlook your slovenliness for the moment," Mistress Anastasia said to Paul's relief. " Right, why do you want to become my slave?" She asked, crossing her knees and wriggling to make herself comfortable whilst awaiting for a lengthy and well-thought-out reply.

"I don't know," Paul replied blushing. He could not help but notice the word 'slave' said repeatedly as if he was in some kind of a surreal dream. "I just have an overwhelming desire to become a slave."

"You don't know?" Mistress Anastasia repeated, raising her voice again. "You come all this way, from Dorset to see me, and you don't know why you are here?" She looked up at the ceiling with an exaggerated expression of disbelief.

"I want very much to become your slave," Paul replied with a little bit of enthusiasm. "I have always dreamt of being a slave to a beautiful Mistress." Mistress smiled at being referred to as beautiful and she slowly warmed to the pathetic little creature before her.

"Yes, but you don't know why you want to serve. Is it to please and pamper me? I am looking for somebody totally selfless to serve me loyally day and night, without any thought to their own comfort and needs. I want somebody reliable, trustworthy and to be totally and absolutely obedient. Is this the type of position you are looking for?"

"Yes, yes," Paul replied.

Mistress Anastasia stood up from her seat and looked down at the nervous little boy.

"You have passed the first part of the interview, now we will retire to my room so I may ask you some more personal questions without the worry of people overhearing. Come, get up and follow me," Mistress Anastasis commanded, and they promptly walked up towards the elevator with Mistress Anastasia taking the lead and the Paul following behind.

Paul could not help but notice what an elegant and refined figure Mistress Anastasia presented as she glided femininely and confidently towards the lift doors. Inside the elevator, nothing was said as the machine glided silently upwards three floors. The lift stopped and a bell chimed as the doors glided open. Mistress Anastasia left first and waited for Paul to follow.

With a smile Mistress Anastasia opened the hotel room door and entered, followed by Paul behind her.

"Take a seat," she said, pointing to a particular chair. "Do you drink coffee?" she asked, picking up the hotel room kettle.

"Yes," Paul mumbled.

"Yes Mistress," Anastasia said, correcting Paul. " We'll start as we mean to go on. Milk, sugar?" She asked.

"Just milk please Mistress," Paul replied, finding the word Mistress alien to say and mumbled the words under his breath.

Anastasia handed Paul his coffee and took her drink and sat on the end of the hotel bed, turning to face her nervous and frightened interviewee.

"Where were we, oh yes," Mistress Anastasia said. "I have five people for an interview today, three no-shows and one very drunk candidate. So, young man, you're the best of the bunch so far, let's keep it up. These hotel rooms, needless to say, are very expensive and I don't want to come back and go through all this interviewing again. I need now to establish if you are worth taking on for a trial period. I was thinking of initially a six months trial to see if you fit in with me and my life."

"Thank you, Mistress," Paul said without prompting. "I will be happy to come for a six-month trial as I have no full-time work at present and between jobs."

" You do realise what I am offering, don't you?" Without pausing for a reply Anastasia continued to say. " I am not looking for kinky sessions. I am not looking for one-offs. This position is not a fantasy, not a game. I am offering you a permanent post, subject to a trial period, a kept position as my 24/7 slave. There are no paid holidays and no pension scheme. You'll have no rights at all, other than to serve me, to the best of your ability." Anastasia put deliberate emphasis on the word slave so Paul would be in no doubt about what he was letting himself in for. How does that sound so far? " She asked.

"Yes, yes, that is what I am looking for," Paul replied with a little hesitancy as he realised the immensity of what he was about to let himself in for.

"Are you absolutely sure this is what you truly want? " Mistress Anastasia asked, looking pensively at Paul as if she wasn't so sure of his answer. "I thought I could detect some doubt in your voice."

"No, No," Paul replied. "I do want to be your slave."

"Then we will go on." Mistress Anastasia replied with an approving smile. " Your duties will be many and varied. They will include housework, all housework," she emphasised. "Not just dusting, sweeping, cleaning, the laundry, ironing, the lot, everything that needs doing in the home will be your responsibility. You will do all the shopping, answer the phone and wait on me hand and foot. Still, sound okay to you? Mistress Anastasia asked. It isn't everybody's cup of tea it takes a special kind of person," Mistress added as an afterthought.

"Yes, I understand what my duties will be."

"Good Mistress Anastasia said a little mockingly. Stand up and put your arms out at your side," she demanded.

"What now, here?" Paul replied, a little shocked by this unexpected request and not really understanding what was required of him.

"Yes, now, right now" Mistress barked, making poor Paul jump with surprise. "Not next week, next year, but right now this second. I don't expect you to ever question what I ask again, you just do what you are told instinctively."

Paul stood almost, losing his balance in the rush, and stretched out his arms at his side.

"That's better. When I give you an order, you don't think about it, you do what I ask immediately without question, do you now understand? I can see you'll need some re-educating."

"Yes, I understand," Paul replied. He found it hard to concentrate with his arms out at his side and he felt them slipping almost immediately through exhaustion.

"Mistress, Mistress, Mistress, when you speak to me, you will always end with the word Mistress. This is an interview but when you begin as my slave every time you forget to show me respect, you'll feel the sting of a cane on your bare backside and I can cane hard, very hard."

"Sorry Mistress," Paul answered, feeling shocked and surprised at the degree of Mistress Anastasia's dominance and assertiveness.

"Shouting at you has made me forget my train of thought," Mistress said, holding her hands to her head as she tried to recall. Oh yes," she announced suddenly, I remember, you'll also be expected to provide personal services. These will include dressing me and helping me with my make-up. You'll also shave and bathe me."

"Lastly," Mistress added with a little smirk. "You'll be expected to use your tongue to bring me to climax as and when I require such relief." Paul nodded that he understood these extra duties which brought a smile to Mistress Anastasia's face.

"I think I might be able to do something with you with some intensive training, when can you start your trial?"

Paul thought about the question for a moment and replied:

"Your arms are slipping, put them back up this instant," Mistress insisted. "I have not told you to put your arms down."

"I could start next week Mistress," Paul answered whilst using all his strength to raise his arm back to where they were.

"Excellent. I will take you for a trial period of six months, if after six months I find you suitable I will give you a permanent collar. You may put your arms down now and sit down. The idea of making you raise your arms at your side is to teach you obedience, obedience will feature very much in your new life."

Paul was so relieved to sit and put his arm back down and into his lap.

"Right, I have to go now," Mistress Anastasis said standing. She passed him some hotel stationary and a pen. "Write your full name and telephone number. I will call you with details of your appointment later and an address to attend on Monday week."

When Paul had finished scribbling down his details Mistress went to the hotel door and opened it.

"You may go now," and with a smile, she held out her hand to shake on their arrangement, and then Paul left after thanking his new Mistress.

Chapter Two.

First day as Mistress's trainee slave.

Paul left the hotel room feeling really pleased with himself and almost skipped and danced down the road to the underground station. On the way home on the train, he wondered what life will be like as Mistress Anastasia's slave. There was a lot to do, he had to give up his part-time job at a newspaper stall and also give notice to the landlord of his bedsit. Then there was packing sorting out his bank accounts and important paperwork to take with him when he goes to Anastasis's home to begin his trial.

As promised Mistress Anastasia telephoned Paul and gave him her address and a time to arrive on his first day. He wasn't to arrive a minute early or a moment late as this will be well frowned upon as he had to learn to be exactly on time. On Monday morning the day of his new appointment, he stood around the corner from Mistress Anastasia's home and studied his watch, so he would arrive bang on eight o clock as instructed.

He walked up to Anastasia's door and watched the second hands-on his watch slowly and arduously tick to the top of the hour and the precise moment the hand reach eight o clock he nervously pressed the doorbell.

At the same moment, Paul was wondering if he was doing the right thing and had a twinge of cold feet. However, Mistress Anastasia must have been looking at her watch too, as she arrived to open her front door almost immediately sealing Paul's fate. She stood there wearing a pink dressing gown and slippers. Paul was surprised to see his Mistress looking so casual and with her hair down.

"That's a good boy, you have arrived exactly on time, I'm impressed. Come in," she urged. "Don't forget to wipe your feet and take off your shoes, or your first job will be cleaning the hall carpet. Follow me."

Mistress sauntered down the hall with her hair flowing side to side. Paul followed in her wake. She stopped at a room and opened the door and stood to the side so Paul could pass into the room.

"Sit in here until I am ready for you." She commanded pointing into the room. Paul did as asked and stepped into the room and Mistress Anastasia shut the door behind him. On his own and bewildered Paul put down his case and found himself a seat on the sofa. Looking around himself, he presumed this was the main living room, but he couldn't be sure as it was clearly a very big house with lots of rooms.

An eternity seemed to pass before Mistress Anastasia returned, by this time Paul's nerves were in shreds, and he was beside himself with panic and dread. Mistress stepped into the room. She was now dressed for the day and had her long hair pinned up in a bun She was a tall lady, a good few inches taller than Paul. She was slim with curvy hips. Her hair, when down, was waist-length dark brown with subtle highlights. Mistress Anastasia was wearing a cream top and cream leather skin-tight trousers. Shockingly, in one hand at her side, she held a black leather riding crop with an inch-long leather tab on the end. Paul couldn't keep his eyes off this formidable implement.

"We had best get you started when you have done some chores we'll stop for a cup of tea and a chat, first through some work. Come with me," she commanded stepping out of the room and waiting for Paul to follow. Paul followed her into the kitchen where Mistress Anastasia filled his arms with cleaning products from under the sink, then she marched him upstairs to the bathroom.

"This is one of three bathrooms, when you have cleaned it to my satisfaction, you may clean the other two. I will leave you to get on. When you have finished, you'll find me in the study downstairs, knock on the door before you enter. " With that comment Mistress, Anastasia was gone, leaving Paul to get on with the task at hand.

At this precise point, Paul had seriously wondered if he was doing the right thing. He had, yet another massive attack of cold feet, and his mind was racing for ways to plan his escape. He kicked himself for finding himself in this situation in the first place.

Paul went out into the corridor and approached the stairs. He could hear Mistress below and froze because cowardly he wanted to escape without Mistress knowing. He was hoping to sneak out of the house unnoticed. Paul couldn't face Mistress's disappointment at him wanting to leave so soon, however, there was no way he could get to the front door and leave without her knowing.

Then Paul decided he would go back to the bathroom and clean it, and plan his escape later when it would be easier to leave undetected. Back to the bathroom, Paul got on with the cleaning. He cleaned everything he could see and when he was satisfied with his work he sensed someone behind him. Paul turned and jumped with shock when he saw Mistress Anastasia standing in the doorway holding the black leather riding crop in both hands, bending it slightly as she spoke.

"My, you are a slow slave. I expected you to be finished ages ago," she said with a final big bend of the riding crop. "Let's see how well you have done. I do expect and demand very high standards from my slave."

Mistress stepped into the room and strutted around the spacious bathroom looking up, and down, and rubbing her finger here and there to detect any dust.

"No, this is no good at all nowhere near the standards I expect, you need to clean the whole bathroom again from top to bottom. Let me show you your errors. There are smudges in the corner of the mirror. Do you see? " She asked, pulling Paul closer by his ear as if he was a naughty child. "You need to get right into the corners with your duster. Now look at the sink, it is clean, on top, but on the underside, it is filthy you hadn't bothered to look. It is exactly the same as the base of the toilet. This needs to be punished, don't you agree? " Mistress Anastasia asked. "If I let you off now, you'll never improve." Paul didn't have much choice but to agree with his Mistress.

"Yes Mistress," Paul mumbled, " I need to be punished."

"I am pleased you agree with me. Excellent decision. Bend over into the bath. " Paul did as he was told and waited for the crop to come crashing down on his backside, which it did three times and very hard strokes they were too.

Although he had his trousers on, the pain was unbearable and his poor buttocks stung and throbbed.

"Clean it all again, I'll be back in half an hour to check again, and don't you think for one moment I won't punish you again if the bathroom hasn't been cleaned properly."

Paul cleaned everything again making a special note of the corners of the mirror. He also cleaned under the toilet and sink. When Mistress returned, she was satisfied with his efforts this time and said a cup of tea awaits him downstairs.

Downstairs, Mistress and Paul retired into the kitchen and she passed him a cup of tea and told him to sit in one of the kitchen table's hard-backed chairs. Paul grimaced as he sat.

"Trouble sitting?" Mistress asked mockingly. "I was being gentle with you as you're new to all this, wait until I punish you properly, then you have something to grimace and moan about."

After a few sips of tea Mistress went on to say:

"By the way, this is your chair, you're not allowed to sit on any other furniture in the house, ever. The furniture is not for slaves, all you may do is clean it. If you have the good fortune to be invited into the living room, you'll sit on the floor. Do you understand, the punishment will be severe if I catch you sitting on anything other than the chair you're sitting in now."

"Yes, I understand," Paul replied, thinking to himself soon he will escape and none of these rules will matter.

"You'll also speak only when spoken to. You'll keep your eyes cast downwards, you're never, to look at Mistress directly unless ordered to do so. Finally, you'll knock on the door when entering a room. Now you have a choice when entering a room with me in it, you can either stand by the door eyes cast downward, legs slightly ajar, hands clasped together neatly in your lap until spoken to, or you can come over to your Mistress and kneel at her side, tight beside me, with eyes cast down with hands neatly in your lap. A lot to absorb, but is that clear slave? "

"Yes Mistress," Paul answered, still mentally planning his escape as he listened.

"Don't worry, Mistress Anastasia said, lowering her voice to a more friendly pitch. You'll soon get the hang of things. I have great expectations for you. Now, when you have finished your cuppa, I'll show you where number two bathroom is so you can make a start. First, though," Mistress added as an afterthought, I'll give you a tour of the house so you can see where everything is. If you get your case from the living room, I will also show you your bedroom."

Paul finished his cup of tea and collected his case and the two of them began a tour of the house, which was much bigger than any house Paul had ever been in before. On the tour, they arrived at Paul's new bedroom.

Mistress Anastasia stepped in first.

"I think you'll be very comfortable here, it is a nice room, a little small, but all a good slave needs."

Paul looked around, the room, it was painted in very deep pink. The bed had a pink headboard with a lacy pink drape, finished off with a light pink duvet and pillows. There was a white dressing table and a hardback chair with a pink base. On the bed were a collection of cuddly toys. The room looked garish to Paul and he hated it instantly.

"It is very girlish and so pink, Paul remarked not liking the room at all. "Can I take out the cuddly toys and pull down the pink drape?"

"No, you cannot," Mistress barked most decisively. "You'll leave the teddy bears and room exactly as it is. I shall check often to make sure nothing has been disturbed. Mistress tutted a bit and added. "You're ungrateful Paul, some slaves have to make do with the kitchen floor to sleep on. Would you prefer the kitchen floor? " Mistress asked. "It can be arranged in an instant."

"No Mistress. I'm sorry."

" I should think so," Anastasia said, accepting his apology. "Don't be so ungrateful, you'll soon learn to love this room."

The two additional bathrooms were bigger than the first one Paul cleaned. One was en suite to Mistress's bedroom. Paul realised he would have to take special care with this room unless he wanted a very sore bottom. The other bathroom had a Jacuzzi in it. Clearly Mistress Anastasia was well-heeled to be able to afford all of this luxury. The house itself must have been worth well over a million Pounds as were most homes in the centre of London. Paul wondered about where she made her fortune or if was it inherited.

Chapter Three.

The Attempted Escape.

Paul got on with his duties, whilst he cleaned and scrubbed and pampered Mistress he was fighting an internal war with himself. It was a tug of war between needing to be submissive and the cultural conditioning he has received since childhood to be assertive and masculine. Most of the time the submissive side of his character won over, but there were days when he questioned what he was doing and the urge to escape and get back to his old life was overpowering.

One such day Paul acted on his need to escape the clutches of his Mistress. Paul spent the morning massaging his Mistress's legs and her most sensitive areas. The pampering and attention had aroused Mistress. The morning was concluded with Paul going down and licking and sucking until Mistress quivered into a succession of climaxes.

Mistress laid back on the bed and propped up a pillow to recover from being pleasured. She ordered Paul to make a coffee and bring it to her in bed. Paul did as he was instructed and brought a cup of coffee to his Mistress. She told him to go on his knees beside her bed.

"I shall have to begin teaching you slave positions. It will be good for you it will help to teach you obedience. There are several positions which you will eventually learn by heart. However, not today, I have to go out this afternoon to meet a friend in town for lunch," Mistress Anastasia told Paul.

"Are you going to restrain me again?" Paul asked. During the first two weeks when Mistress left the house, Paul was tied either on the bed or in a hard-backed chair until Mistress Anastasia returned.

"The last two weeks I have been on vacation from work," Mistress began to explain, "so I could dedicate my time to give you some initial training and help you settle in. Now, however, I have to go back to work Monday morning. I can't keep you chained up forever as you won't be able to perform your duties efficiently whilst I am away from the house, so I shall have to put my trust in you that you won't run away."

"I won't run away Mistress," Paul replied, perhaps not too convincingly. Mistress frowned slightly as she worried about the conviction of that sentence and then replied:

"We shall see. Not only might you run away you might also take the silver with you, so it is all a matter of trust. If I can't trust my slave, who can I trust? " Mistress Anastasia paused and thought a bit whilst sipping her coffee. "When I go out this afternoon I will give you plenty of chores to do and the front door will be left unlocked."

Paul went back about his duties and Mistress Anastasia went up to her bedroom to change and get ready for her afternoon out. When she finished dressing she came downstairs. She was dressed in a plumb-coloured midi dress, a white cardigan, and white strappy sandals. She found Paul sitting in the kitchen as he had finished some of his chores and was having a tea break.

Mistress Anastasia stood at the kitchen door with hands on her hips and blurted:

"Well?"

"Well, what Mistress?" Paula answered a little confused.

"Don't you stand up for your Mistress? Weren't you brought up to stand for a woman when she enters the room?"

Paul jumped to his feet and stood to attention.

"I won't stand for this slovenly behaviour, when I come home, I will introduce you to my cane. Being gentle with you isn't working and I think you'll profit from more discipline. You should stand up for all women who enter the room not just your Mistress any women, it is common courtesy. "

"Sorry Mistress, I will try harder," Paul assured Mistress Anastasia.

"You will trust me, you will," Mistress agreed. "Right, I am off out now and should be back before 6 pm. I expect you to have dinner cooked in anticipation of my return. I have left a list of what I want for dinner on the stove."

With those words, Mistress Anastasia turned and headed off down the corridor, stopping to pick up her handbag and coat from a peg in the hall. She left with a loud slam of the heavy front door behind her.

Paul didn't like the thought of receiving the cane, on Mistress's return and decided to run away now today. He waited though to be sure Mistress had actually left and wasn't about to return because of something she had forgotten. So he got on with his chores just in case she came back. After about half an hour Paul was satisfied his Mistress was truly away for the afternoon. He rushed up the stairs and hurriedly packed his bags, not taking any care, he just screwed up his clothes and chucked them into his case.

When packed he took his cases back down into the hall and put them down, as now he didn't feel so determined to leave as he was a few moments ago. Paul knew once he was out the door, there was no going back, the deed had been done. He wouldn't be able to undo his actions or change his mind. Now was the time to be sure of his choices. That familiar tug of war had returned, now he was in two minds, whether or not to proceed or take his cases back upstairs. Paul decided to sit on one of the hall chairs while he battled with his indecisiveness.

As he pondered he heard the front door open and in stepped Mistress Anastasia. Paul sprung to his feet in shock and surprise at seeing her return so early.

"I saw you, you were sitting on a chair which is forbidden. We'll discuss this again later when I get my cane. My girlfriend didn't show up. Oh, I'm so annoyed after going all that way into town. It is good I have a bottom to cane later to take away my pent-up frustrations, Mistress said smiling at Paul. "Go and make me a coffee, I'm parched. I'll see you in the kitchen in a moment. Paul shot off to the kitchen to put on the kettle.

"Paul," Mistress shouted from the hall.

Paul left the kitchen and returned to the hall to see what was troubling Mistress.

"Yes Mistress," Paul said whilst wiping his hands with a tea towel.

"What is this?" Mistress said, with a trembling hand pointing at his case on the hall floor. "Are you going to leave me?"

"No Mistress, no Mistress," Paul pleased clasping his hands together as in a prayer.

"Then explain why you have brought your cases downstairs if you're not leaving me?" Mistress Anastasia asked with disappointment in her voice. "What else can it possibly mean?" she inquired.

"I am sorry Mistress, I'm so sorry. I was going to run away, but I changed my mind and was going to take my case back upstairs." Paul said, somewhat pathetically, as he goes down on his knees and begs for forgiveness.

"Are you sure you were not about to go or did I just interrupt your plans by returning early?" Mistress asked standing over the pathetic snivelling creature on his knees. Anastasia's disappointment in Paul had brought out her German accent as she spoke and seemed visibly shocked and saddened by his actions. Paul was shocked by her response and hadn't imagined how upset she would be discovering he was about to leave.

"Go on, pick up your case and go. Leave now before I get really angry." Mistress commanded, pointing to the front door with a trembling hand.

"No Mistress, please, please give me another chance. I will be a good slave I promise and I'll never attempt to leave again. Please let me stay," Paul pleaded.

Mistress Anastasia stood silently whilst she pondered over Paul's entreaties. Mistress finally spoke and said:

"I am very upset and disappointed in you. Go and stand in that corner whilst I think about what I am going to do with you. I am sick of the sight of you, go into the corner now before I change my mind and take you to the door by the scruff of your next and sling you out."

"Thank you, Mistress, thank you," Paul said as he scurried off into the corner.

"Put your hands on your head and stay there perfectly still until I call you and I mean perfectly still," Mistress added as she left him in the hallway to go and get changed into something more relaxing.

Paul stood there in the corner with his hands on his head for an eternity. He seemed to be standing for hours and hours, although in reality it was only about two hours in total. The boredom was immense, there was nothing to look at or do, but to fill his mind with thoughts and regrets. He was in the corner for so long, his legs were getting numb and he wondered if Mistress had actually forgotten he was there until finally, he heard her approach.

"You can come out of the corner now and go to the toilet and then come straight back here," Mistress said in a cold monotone, her continued disappointment evident in her voice.

Paul ran off to the toilet as he was certainly busting. The relief was exquisite and felt much better until he remembered now he had to return to face a very unhappy Mistress.

Chapter Four

Second Chance.

Paul gingerly and quietly went back to find Mistress Anastasia. He found her in the kitchen making herself a sandwich.

"You should be doing this," she said, but I was too hungry to wait for you to return. Would you like a sandwich?"

"No thank you, Mistress," Paul replied, as he was in Mistress's bad books, asking for a sandwich seemed a bit too much under the circumstances, although he was actually quite hungry.

"Well, you are getting one, you haven't eaten in hours. Take this one, I'll make another," she said, handing Paul her sandwich.

Paul thanked Mistress and took a cheese sandwich from her and took a bite while he waited for Mistress's next command.

"Sit on your chair," Mistress barked. "We need to discuss what we are going to do with you."

Paul drew up his special chair and sat at the kitchen table. Mistress finished making her sandwich and joined him at the table. She quietly took a few bites before speaking:

"We have a trust problem, Paul." Mistress stopped to take another bite. "God I'm hungry," she added. "If I keep you on here, how can I trust you won't do this to me again? Perhaps next time you'll actually go and leave me without a slave which will be very inconvenient."

"I won't try to leave again," Paul reassured Mistress. "I've learned my lesson I do want to be your slave, I'm sure of that now. I needed a jolt to make me realise how lucky I am to have you for my Mistress."

"Well, Paul, I am not so sure, and Monday I go back to work. I need someone here to keep the house clean and tidy. It will be more than just an inconvenience if you left again. I will have to take more time off to find a new slave and my work will suffer badly."

"I'll be good, Mistress, I promise I won't try and run away again. They both sat silently while they ate their sandwiches. Then Mistress stood up and went to the kitchen door.

"Now we have finished our sandwiches come with me," Mistress said breaking the silence. They both stepped back out into the hall.

"Pick up your cases and follow me." Mistress Anastasia waited for Paul to pick up his cases and he followed her upstairs. They stopped at the room beside Paul's bedroom. Mistress got a key from her pocket and unlocked the door and they both entered. It was a box room and had all manner of things neatly stored in boxes and cases.

"Put down your suitcase on the floor and undress, everything off, the lot down to your birthday suit," Mistress demanded and put her arms on her hips as she waited impatiently for Paul to strip.

"Undress?" Paul asked as he began to unbelt.

"Yes, what is it about the word undress you don't understand? Now undress quickly before I get very annoyed with you. Remember you're now on probation."

When Paul was stripped off and felt naked in more than just the physical sense, he waited for Mistress's next command.

"Now fold up your clothes and put them in your case and put the case neatly with the other boxes. Paul nervously did as he was told and put his case on top of some other cases in the room. They left the room and Mistress locked the door behind them.

"Now if you get the urge to leave me and escape from my clutches, you'll have to go nude. That should make sure you're still here when I come home at night," Mistress said with a self-satisfied smile.

"There is another matter to attend to, your shoddy work earlier today and sitting on an unauthorised chair. I shall go and find my cane, you'll enjoy being introduced to my cane. I call it my little stinger. You can go and wait in the living room and I will be with you shortly to introduce you both."

This was to be Paul's second punishment and he was very apprehensive about it as he made his way down the stairs. Mistress Anastasia who was out of sight shouted from behind him:

"And when you go into the living room find yourself a corner to stand in and wait with your hands on your head until I arrive.

Paul did as he was told and stood in the corner of the living room. He was remiss about putting his hands on his head as he panicked about his forthcoming caning. This was only the second time Mistress had cause to punish him and also he had never experienced the cane before, but he had heard stories about the cane being the most painful implement of them all and he was about to find out if the rumours were true.

Paul heard the living room door squeak open and he quickly placed his hands on his head before he thought Mistress had noticed.

"Too late," Mistress Anastasia remarked. "I saw you put your hands on your head, that will be an extra two stokes of the cane for this error. Paul started to turn but was quickly put in his place.

"Who told you to move," Mistress barked, "that's another two extra strokes. You stay exactly where you are until I tell you otherwise," she said, adding, "I'm not ready for you yet."

Paul heard some shuffling noises and the odd swishing sound of the cane. He seemed to be standing there for an eternity, he didn't want to wait any longer, he wanted to get the punishment over and done with.

"Right you can come out of the corner now and come over here." Mistress Anastasia ordered.

Paul gingerly stepped over to Mistress's side. Mistress pulled him by his wrist to the end of the sofa and pushed him over the arm of the seat. Once bend over Mistress ordered him to tip-toe.

"Let's get this over with, as I am getting hungry again and want you to make a start on dinner,"

Mistress informed him. Before Paul had a chance to absorb what Mistress had said down came the cane. The pain was unbearable it was like an electric shock and before the pain subsided down came the cane again and again.

"Twelve strokes plus four extras," Mistress said whilst bringing down the cane for the third time.

Chapter Four.

Getting cold.

Several weeks went by and Paul had pretty much accepted his lot as Mistress Anastasia's slave. His thoughts of escaping subsided, partly due to getting used to and accepting his role and partly because working in the nude and having no access to clothes prevented such thoughts. The first few days of working without any clothes he felt really odd and vulnerable, After a few days, he got used to being nude and barely noticed, except when he was cooking as he got scolded by splashes a lot more than when he was wearing clothes.

However, as the summer months turned to autumn and eventually winter, the heating in Mistress Anastasia's house wasn't sufficient to stop Paul from shivering at times. Mistress was warm enough with clothes on but poor Paul would freeze at times and his whole body would be covered in goosebumps. He was frightened of succumbing to illness and knew he would have to speak to Mistress about it.

Paul was waiting for the right moment when Mistress Anastasia was in an exceptionally good mood to broach the question of him having some clothes before he caught a chill. Paul didn't need to worry, as one day when serving Mistress coffee and biscuits, she noticed goosebumps on his bare arms. Mistress Anastasia grabbed one of Pauls's hands and held it in hers. Paul immediately felt the heat radiate from Mistress's soft hands to his hand and he didn't want her to let go.

"You're cold, in fact, I would say you're freezing," Mistress exclaimed, quite shocked by her discovery. "Um, what are we to do with you?"

"Yes Mistress, " Paul replied. "I have been cold for a while now and the only time I feel warm is when I go to bed. Can I wear some clothes, please? " He pleaded. "I won't escape I promise. I have learned my lesson now."

"I don't know slave," Mistress replied eying him up and down as she thought about the problem. "I'm frightened you'll run off again once you know you can, the temptation may be too much for you. I can't be without a slave now

I have too much work on at the moment, Besides I have spent a lot of time and trouble training you," she added. "You're my investment and I can't let my investment try and escape again."

"Please Mistress before I get a chill and become ill. An ill slave is no good to you," Paul reminded his Mistress.

"Yes, you are right a poorly slave would be a burden I can do without." Mistress stopped talking to think. "Right in the short term, I will go now and turn the heating up a couple of degrees, that should help a bit until I decide what to do with you."

Mistress left Paul in the living room while she went off to the kitchen to find the central heating thermostat. When Mistress Anastasia returned to the living room, she stopped and gave Paul yet another look up and down and appeared to be thinking hard about the problem. With a little bit of a smirk, she said:

"Yes, it might work you're about a size 16," she muttered to herself. "You'll hate it, right follow me," Mistress demanded, and off they went upstairs to Mistress's bedroom. Mistress went into the bedroom first and Paul stood close to the bedroom door and watched Mistress Anastasia go straight to a walk-in closet. She stood a few inches into the closet and started sifting through some clothes on a rack. Paul reminded himself of Anastasia's words "you'll hate it and being a size 16", and almost guessed what was going to happen next.

"I know it's here somewhere," Mistress muttered. "I had a slave once who also left unexpectedly and she left a lot of her clothes behind in her rush to go. I have kept them somewhere as I thought they might come in handy one day."

Paul was quick to note the pronoun " she and her" used by his Mistress and began to feel a little uncomfortable as he could see all the clothes on the rack appeared to only be women's clothes.

"Ah, here we are," said Mistress Anastasia announced, holding up a French Maid's dress for Paul to see. It was a purple dress and to go with it Mistress found a frilly purple petticoat, choker, black apron, and a little purple flower hair band.

"Not for me, I hope Mistress, besides it, looks too small." Paul objected turning to leave the room.

"Stop," Mistress commanded. "Think about what you're doing, if you disobey me once more and leave the room you can go and pack.

Besides," Mistress Anastasia added in a lowered voice. "The dress has an elasticated waist and is one size fits all. It will look lovely on you and it is appropriate for your position as my servant. Although I will enjoy seeing you in it, you'll not be wanting to walk the streets of London wearing it and that is the object of this exercise to keep you in the home when I am away."

Mistress paused to think for a moment and then said. "You have three choices and you have to make one, right, now before we leave this room. Choice one, you can pack and go this instant and be gone with you. Choice two, you can continue to work in the nude, but it will soon be winter and more uncomfortable for you. Choice three, you put on this dress, look pretty for your Mistress and be warm and comfortable while you work."

Paul stood there as his mind raced over the options presented by Mistress. He didn't want to leave and he didn't want to be cold all the time. Paul looked at the dress almost wanting it as he knew the dress, although flimsy would keep him so much warmer than he is now, however, he couldn't stop reminding himself it was nonetheless a dress for sissies.

"Come on," Mistress Anastasia urged. "I need a decision now, I don't have all day. It is a simple choice," Mistress added looking at her wristwatch. "Make up your mind now, or go and pack and be gone with you."

"Okay, I'll wear the dress Mistress," Paul replied begrudgingly. Mistress Anastasia smiled as she knew, in reality, Paul's choices were limited and she didn't think he would choose to leave.

"Then come here and let's try it on for size, as I say it is one size fits all, so it should be alright," Mistress said beckoning Paul to come over to where she was standing. She slipped the dress over Paul's head and pulled it down into shape.

"Yes, that's fine, you look a picture, so sweet," Mistress said approvingly as she looked at Paul. "Now take it off you'll need more than just the dress. I can't have you walking around looking like a man in a frock, we need to sort you out properly. I think with a little effort you'll make a very passable female maid."

Paul took the maid's dress off as Mistress Anastasia rummaged through her wardrobes for other items of clothing. First, she found a red bra and matching panties and put them on the bed. Then she found a pair of used black pantie hose and some black flat shoes. In another cupboard, she found a platinum blond wig.

"None of these things will fit you well, but they will do for now to get you started. I can't see you running off when I am finished with you. Right," Mistress Anastasia added, "let's put all this on and while you are doing that, I will collect up a bag of makeup for you to use."

It was true, none of the clothing fitted Paul very well, but nevertheless, he looked the part of a French maid when Mistress had finished with him.

"Don't worry, we will get some clothes to fit you properly later, this will do for now. You will also need a new name, can't call you Paul looking like this, can we," Mistress said, eying Paul up and down. "I suppose Paula is the obvious choice, yes, I have decided after some thought, we will call you Paula from now on."

Paula had been born. She was given a bag of makeup to take to her room and as a finishing touch just before she left Mistress Anastasia, smothered her in perfume. Then it was back to her normal chores and drudgery dressed in her new outfit. All thoughts of running away had now vanished forever, there was no way Paula was going to run into the street looking the way she did. Mistress was now safe with her new devoted slave and Paula was warm and cosy in her new clothes. It was a win, win situation.

As the weeks went by Mistress Anastasia exchanged items of Paula's clothing for something better fitting and more appropriate. Mistress Anastasia hadn't realised how much she was enjoying transforming her slave into a compliant feminine maid. She really enjoyed choosing clothes for Paula and loved watching her squirm with humiliation as she tried new things on. Mistress Anastasia was very astute and also realised Paula too was becoming hooked on her new ego, although Paula wouldn't admit it. Mistress Anastasia knew she wanted the transformation and craved the added attention she was getting from her Mistress.

Slowly Paula had built up a wardrobe of clothes for all occasions.

Mistress Anastasia was happy now that Paula had given up all desire to leave and was accepting her lot as Madam's servant girl. Paula looked more convincing, pretty, and feminine as the weeks passed.

Chapter Five.

Paula's feminisation.

Most evenings when Paula had finished her chores and wasn't under punishment, she would be allowed to join Mistress in the living room to read, relax, watch television and chat about the day. Mistress Anastasia realised how important it was for Paula to have some downtime, it helped with Mistress and slave bonding.

One particular day Paula came into the living room and slouched into the sofa and opened a book to read. Mistress observed the rather masculine way Paula sat down and realised that a course of feminine deportment was needed if Paula was ever going to ever pass as a female. There was much to be done and Mistress decided to make a start. This would include walking in heels, sitting, standing, and a host of other activities that would make Paula appear more feminine.

"Paula," Mistress Anastasia said, causing Paula to come to attention and put her book down to listen. "You're a lady now, it is time for you to start behaving like one. In the evenings from now on, instead of reading books, we will have a couple of hours of feminine deportment in an effort to help you act and behave more femininely. We will make a start this evening, put your book down and stand up."

Paula did as she was told and placed the book beside her and stood up.

"Girls don't flop into their seats, they sit gracefully. Watch me," Mistress added standing up herself. Mistress Anastasia smoothed her skirt and lowered herself into her armchair and placed her hands demurely onto her knees. "Note I have kept my knees and ankles together during the entire movement. Now you try it."

Paula awkwardly copied Mistress failing to keep her knees together, she sensed immediately that Mistress wasn't happy with her efforts. Mistress without any explanation got up and left the room, quickly returning with her favourite riding crop.

"I find, the occasional flick with the crop on the buttocks improves the slave's concentration when she isn't grasping certain concepts," Mistress Anastasia said bending the crop to make her point. "Shall we try again, stand and sit as I demonstrated to you?"

It was a painful couple of hours of tuition, but Mistress was committed to turning Paula into the perfect lady if it was the last thing she would ever do. It was her mission to turn Paula into something indistinguishable from a real refined woman. The only problem was Paula was a reluctant subject of all this new attention.

Paula's evenings from that day onward were filled with lady deportment activities. Paula had no idea how much went into behaving femininely. The evenings were set aside for walking, standing, sitting, and even eating in a femininely acceptable way. It was all about changing Paula's mindset and removing all vestiges of masculinity from her mind. It was a long process of reprogramming Paula's mind, so she not only looked feminine, but felt it in every respect.

Paula learned that walking required two separate skills, walking in flat shoes and walking with heels. When Paula progressed to heels, she spent many an evening finding her balance and was taught to step with the heel first, then down on the sole, and to slightly walk one foot in front of the other. Paula spent many an evening walking up and down the living room floor to the sound of Mistress Anastasia flicking the riding crop through the air, to encourage speedy progress. Paula also had to learn how to walk up and down stairs in heels. Tripping over which Paula sometimes did during these practice sessions warranted going over the arm of the sofa for twelve well-delivered strokes of the crop. They weren't gentle strokes either and would have Paula yelping and begging Mistress Anastasia to stop.

Soon Paula mastered the arts of behaving femininely save one, eating. Paula had years of bad habits to overcome and was used to scoffing her food to consume it whilst it was still hot. To eat slowly and chew every bit went against years of bad eating.

This amused Mistress Anastasia as it gave her plenty of opportunities to use her skills with the riding crop, and recently she had graduated to use a senior dragon cane. Mistress loved to see the welts appear in neat rows on Paula's bare and vulnerable buttocks.

Paula was also put on a salad diet to bring down her weight to a more acceptable size and lose the slight, but nevertheless masculine beer belly. A pretty slender girl Paula was going to become no matter how much it hurt, Paula that is.

Once a week, to Paula's embarrassment, a young lady would call at the house to give her laser treatment to rid Paula of her manly body hair. Not that Paula was particularly hairy anyway, but she had too much hair for Mistress Anastasia's liking. Also, she needed to lose the five o'clock shadow, to look more convincing as a woman. Paula was also taught feminine mannerisms and behaviours which are very different from that of men. It all ended with speech therapy and finally, after a long and arduous year, Paula looked and sounded like a woman without any hormone treatment.

Not only was Paula transformed into an acceptable lady, but she was also during the year taught to serve Mistress and all her needs domestic or sexual. Female deportment came into its own when Paula was serving Mistress in an evening. She was taught to stand demurely by the side of the living room door legs together and elbows tight to her side and hands crossed in her lap until summoned to attend to Mistress.

When delivering a tray of beverages Paula once again had to stand with her legs together and place the tray down without bending her knees. Paula was meticulous in all her actions as she hated being punished in front of the guests. Mistress, however, loved witnessing Paula's embarrassment and watching her squirm when she was told sometimes in front of strangers to bend over and touch her toes and wait for the sting of the cane.

Paula's feminine transition lacked one thing, she had no sexual experience with men. Mistress Anastasia thought hard about this problem and felt Paula too needed some sexual release. No way was Paula going to be allowed sex with a woman, other than the services she provided for Anastasia. Unknown to Paula Mistress Anastasia began a hunt for a suitable man to break Paula in, and introduce the delights Paula has so far been deprived of.

One evening the doorbell rang and Paula was sent to answer it. This was unusual, for in the evening, Mistress usually answered the door herself. However, she told Paula she was expecting a visitor and off Paula went to answer the door. She came back with a man in his late forties, tall and quite muscular for his age. Mistress Anastasia shook his hand.

"I only have an hour or so," he said, looking at his watch. I need to be somewhere else."

"Right, well, we had better get on." Mistress Anastasia said. "This is Paula, the person you have come to see tonight. Paula this is Simon I have hired him for the evening."

"Hired him?" Paula asked, wondering if she had misheard.

"Yes, yes," Mistress replied without qualification. " Now come here Paula and kneel."

Paula was made to kneel right in front of the man, inches from his feet as he stood there.

"Simon has something nice for you to suck," Anastasia said as he unbuttoned his trousers, then out popped a very large, very erect penis.

"You know what to do," Mistress said.

Paula looked up at Mistress with pleading eyes, but she took no notice of her silent entreaties and guided Paula's head towards the penis before retiring to a nearby seat to watch. Paula sucked and sucked and after twenty minutes Simon gushed into her mouth with a satisfied groan.

"I must go now," Simon said, buttoning up his trousers.

"How well did Paula do?" Asked Mistress as she guided Simon to the door.

"Very good, but she needs a little more practice," Simon said, looking back at Paula with a smile, who was still on her knees.

"Then we must invite you again," Mistress Anastasia said, showing the man out of the front door.

Chapter Six

Growing closer.

As time went by Mistress Anastasia became very fond of her slave Paula and found her indispensable as she managed all the domestic work, freeing Mistress up to spend more time running her business. Despite Paula's excellent practical help, she was also a companion, and Mistress would sometimes share her innermost feelings with Paula in the knowledge Paula would be perfectly discreet.

Of course, this closeness was within the boundaries and confines of being a Mistress and slave. Nevertheless, the relationship worked well and they complimented each other. However, there was also a need for Mistress Anastasia to maintain the discipline to keep Paula firmly at her pace and submissive. Mistress had a knack for bringing Paula down to earth when she least expected it.

Kinky parties were a good time for Mistress to remind Paula of her inferior position in the household. Mistress Anastasia held a kinky party once a month and had her attic converted into a dungeon for the entertainment of her guests. The dungeon consisted of suspension racks, wooden handcrafted stocks, a spanking bench and racks, and rows of whips and canes of all sizes and shapes. There was also a cupboard filled with dildos, strap ons and other toys for her guests' usage. It was as well equipped as most commercial dungeons.

Mistress Anatasia's gatherings were very popular and sometimes there were as many as fifty guests who would attend. They wouldn't all go to the dungeon at once and were dispersed around the house.

Paula's duties were fairly predictable and she would be a maid for the evening and would take coats at the door and provide guests with drinks as the evening progressed. Paula would be dressed in a black satin maid's outfit, heels, and seamed stockings. It was mostly couples who attended Mistress Anastasia's parties and would congregate in the living room for drinks and one by one a couple or two would disappear up into the attic for a session of play and then return downstairs after for more socialising and drinks.

Throughout most of the evening Paula would either be serving drinks or in the kitchen washing up, rarely would she go up to the attic, unless she was due to be punished for some offence earlier in the day.

At one such party, whilst at the sink knee-deep in dirty plates and glasses, Mistress Anastasia appeared and told Paula to stop what she was doing, wipe her hands dry and go straight up to the attic.

With a respectful curtsy, Paula wiped her hands and made her way through party-goers, and went upstairs to the attic as she was told, when she entered the room, she saw a lady tied down on a table having sex with a man with an enormous penis and another female being whipped on a frame nearby by her husband.

Paula found a corner out of the way and watched the proceedings until her Mistress arrived. Mistress Anastasia arrived a few moments later and glanced around the room until her eyes met Paula's.

"Ah, there you are Paula, come here and go on your knees," she commanded, pointing to a spot directly in front of her. Paula obeyed instantly, came over to her Mistress and gave a quick curtsy, and dropped to her knees in the manner she had been taught.

"You have been a very clumsy girl. You have spilt drinks tonight and have broken two wine glasses. " Mistress paused for effect and to gauge Paula's reaction, but Paula had her face cast down whilst she was being admonished. "And what happens to naughty girls?" Mistress Anastasia asked, knowing the reply.

"Naughty girls are punished severely," Paula replied meekly without taking her eyes from the ground.

"Yes, naughty girls are punished severely. Stand up and come with me," she said, walking over to the far side of the attic, where there was one of the handcrafted wooden stocks.

"I am not sure what punishment to give you, so I am putting you in here until I have made up my mind," Mistress said, opening the stock so Paula could rest her head and arms in the purpose-made slots. Then she closed the stock giving Paula a peck on the forehead and said. "I'll be back for you later my dear."

Mistress seemed to be gone forever and rejoined her guests and for a while forgot all about Paula up in the attic. Soon the attic was empty of people and Paula was all alone in the wooden stock feeling very stiff, lonely, and uncomfortable. Eventually, when Mistress remembered Paula was left in the stocks, she returned, but she was not alone, she brought about twenty guests with her to witness poor Paula's impending punishment.

A small table was brought into the centre of the room and Mistress laid out several implements which included a crop, flogger, and cane amongst over cruel-looking objects. They were assembled in a row to be used in order, one after the other until she reached the most painful, the cane at the end.

Paula was released from the wooden stock and brought over to the centre of the room before she had the chance to stretch and recover from her confines.

"Undress, everything off Paula and don't keep us waiting for it is getting late." Mistress stood back and patiently waited for hapless Paula to strip off her clothes and neatly fold and put them on a nearby chair. Then Paula stood, only in her bra arms folded nervously waiting for what was going to come next. Mistress then proceeded to put a blindfold on Paula and handcuffed her hands behind her back.

"Doesn't she have a nice body," Mistress Anastasia said, circling and inspecting her victim as she squirmed. She rubbed and caressed Paula's bottom with her hand as she spoke. "Paula has looked after herself well," Concluding with a loud slap on Paula's bottom, Mistress Anastasia walked to the table and selected the first implement a wooden paddle. The slaps of the paddle had Paula wincing as she realised she was in for a long and painful session with her Mistress.

Next was a large leather flogger which made more noise than pain and gave Paula a short respite. After the flogger came a single-tailed whip which stung and had Paula leaping in the air and she had to be told repeatedly to keep still. Then came the riding crop to add to Paula's agony.

"Now to finish off with the cane," Mistress said, demonstrating its swish qualities to Paula and the audience. "I think for this punishment we will have you bent over a spanking bench."

To help out two members of the audience dragged over a spanking bench to the centre of the room and Paula bent over the contraption. The two helpers helped to strap Paula down so she was unable to move at all.

Paula endured twenty strokes of the cane, which had her in a flood of tears, the pain was exquisite and surpassed all the other implements that were used on her that evening.

Mistress Anastasia admired her workmanship and run her hands down the swollen cane welts whilst Paula's bottom stung and tears rolled down her cheeks. Then she was released from the spanking bench and made to stand to attention in front of her Mistress.

"I hope that has taught you a lesson to be more careful with the dishes in future," Mistress said, indicating she wanted Paula to go back down on her knees which she did instantly.

"Attention everybody," Mistress shouted above the dim of chit-chat. I have an announcement to make to you all. Paula has successfully just finished her six months probation as my personal slave. " Everybody clapped and cheered at Paula's achievement. When the clapping subsided Mistress said to Paula:

"Paula you have served me for the last six months and during that time we have got to know each other well. I have been very pleased with your service, although there were some initial hick-ups. I think the time has come to ask you, do you wish to become my permanent slave and serve me for the rest of your life?"

"Yes Mistress," Paula said without hesitation. "Please may I spend the rest of my life as your slave?"

" Yes, you may be my slave for life," Mistress replied approvingly and then turned to the small gathering. Attention everybody you have a cordial welcome to Paula's collaring ceremony here at my home one month from today."

Everyone present said they will be delighted to come and began applauding again.

Chapter Seven.

The Big Preparation.

Mistress Anasastasia's parties, provided Paula with light relief, as life was, by and large, consisted of repetitive domestic drudgery. Paula's life was without a doubt hard and she had given up much most people take for granted. Paula had no days off, she was on duty every day and every night. She also had no cash of her own and all her needs were decided and provided by Mistress Anastasia. Paula also had no choice in what she wore and was mostly confined to the home and rarely went out unless to shop with her Mistress. Lastly, all her friends were provided by her Mistress and had none she could call her own. She would also lose out on ever having children or a relationship of her own. Paula's choice to become a lifetime slave was a bigger decision than one might have thought at first glance.

The morning after the party, the one where Mistress announced the impending collaring ceremony, Paula was busy cleaning the kitchen. She looked up from scrubbing the kitchen floor to see Mistress's patent heels and stocking-clad legs standing astride in front of her.

"When you have finished the kitchen, Paula, come into the living room as we need to have a chat about the announcement I made last night."

"Yes Mistress," Paula replied, " I am almost done here, I'll be along shortly."

"Good, good," Mistress answered. "Right, carry on with your work and come to me when you are finished."

Paula finished working in the kitchen, washed her hands, and straightened her clothes before knocking on the living room door which was closed.

"Come in, Paula," Mistress shouted from within the room.

Paula stepped in and approached Mistress with a respectful curtsey, which seem to get Mistress's approval as she smiled back.

"Come and take a seat next to me," Mistress Anastasia said, patting the sofa at her side. Paula sat and when she had made herself comfortable Mistress continued to speak. "I've changed my mind, we won't have your collaring here in the house, it is too small for all the guests. This morning I hired a fetish club in the centre of London for my exclusive use for the night." Mistress Anastasia paused for Paula to absorb the information then said:

"I telephoned around this morning and spoke to various Dommes, Mistresses, and Masters and I discovered there are quite a few collaring coming up and we decided to hold all the ceremonies on the same evening. It will make it more of an occasion and it will help to bring the costs down. So it is going to be quite a night, but as I am financing most of it, our collaring ceremony will be the main event of the evening. So my girl we need to do something very special as it will be a once-in-a-lifetime event."

Paula sat up in her seat and listened without saying a word, but she was nevertheless clearly intrigued and wanted to know more.

"First, though the most essential ingredient of a collaring ceremony is the collar itself. Paula, have you any thoughts on the type of collar you would like?

"No Mistress," Paula replied. " I haven't really had a chance to think about it since last night."

"Yes, I understand," Mistress Anastasia agreed. "It is something for you to consider. What you need to understand is, you'll be wearing the collar permanently, all day, all night, and every day, so ideally, it needs to be a collar you'll like to wear." Mistress stopped speaking to give Paula a chance to think about it.

"I could choose a collar for you, most Mistresses do. However, I want you to have the collar you have chosen. For example, do you want a leather collar or a metal collar? A thin collar or a wider one. What colour would you like? " There are so many to choose from."

Mistress picked up a catalogue from a table at the side of the sofa and passed it to Paula.

"This catalogue has hundreds of different collars of all shapes and sizes. I personally the leather ones that can be locked with a key, but take no notice of me, it is your neck, your choice." Paula flicked through the magazine. "You can take your time, but I would like you to choose a collar today so I can order it in good time for the ceremony. So my girl, get choosing from the catalogue I have just given you. Don't worry about your chores, they can wait, sit here and pick your collar first. No rush, take your time."

Paula began to look at the catalogue in earnest and after several minutes of flicking through the pages she looked up at her Mistress and said pointing to a suitable collar:

"Can I have this one please Mistress?"

Mistress followed Paula's finger and saw a dainty purple leather collar with a small nickel-plated heart-shaped lock.

"That's a very good choice, I like it too, I will order it today for you," Mistress said with a smile as she was more than pleased with Paula's choice. "Now, you may go back to work, we will have another chat later this afternoon. Go on, off you go to your chores." Mistress urged as Paula seemed slow to move from her seat.

Paula returned to her chores and later that afternoon after lunch, Mistress summoned Paula back to the living room for another chat about her plans for the collaring. Paula was invited to sit by his Mistress on the sofa as she did earlier in the morning.

"I have been busy all day arranging this and that for our big day. The club I have hired for the night is called the Apple Tree Fetish Club near The Shard in Central London. Believe me," Mistress Anastasia added excitedly, "it is a top location very exclusive, we're very lucky to be able to book this club. It is ours for us and our friends for the whole evening, no one can come in off the street without an invitation. I have also ordered your collar and lock and we should have that in a week or so, well in advance of the collaring."

"I can't wait to see my collar," Paula said, sharing some of Mistress's excitement. Paula's enthusiasm pleases Mistress Anastasia and she became more and more infused with the project as they fed off each other.

"Although you chose the collar you won't see it until the night of the collaring, it would be bad luck for you to see it any sooner," Mistress warned, to Paula's disappointment. "I called you in here this afternoon as we will need to discuss what we are going to wear in the evening. It's going to be a big advent and we'll both need new clothes for the occasion. Also," Mistress added we need to think about what the ceremony will consist of. What sort of ceremony do we want? We will want our collaring to put all the other collaring that evening into the pail."

"We are not going to decide today, are we?" Paula asked.

"On no, the collaring is too important for us to rush into anything. I just want us to start the creative juices to come up with some ideas. I am open to your ideas Paula, don't think I won't consider any thoughts you might have on the subject. The ceremony isn't mine alone, it is ours. However, there will be some surprises for you and these will be kept secret until the night. "

Mistress Anastasia and Paula descended into deep thought and sat silently on the sofa while they each mulled things over in their mind.

"I have the seeds of an idea. I will have to contact all the other couples to be collared to get their broad agreement. I was thinking of a competition where all the submissives and slaves to be collared will have to prove their worth to their Mistress or Master. Only those who pass all the tests will go on to be collared."

"What if I fail the tests? " Paula asked despondently.

"You won't," Mistress said decisively. "If you do, God help you my girl your life won't be worth the effort. I was thinking of several tasks each submissive will have to perform to show their submissiveness, obedience, and loyalty. Each Mistress can help choose the severity of the tests to suit their submissives. There might be special deportment tests for 'sissies' like yourself Paula to prove you are a truly committed sissy. It's going to be a fun evening. These are only ideas at present, nothing is set in stone, and they all need to be thought through." Mistress concluded before sending Paula off to start preparing dinner.

Over the next week, Paula chose a new frock from a catalogue. The dress she chose was a white midi dress, it could have been taken for a wedding dress except it had a light purple collar and waist belt. Mistress immediately ordered the frock on Paula's behalf. Paula was also told she will be placed on a 600-calorie diet for the next three weeks to help her lose some of the excess weight around her tummy. Of course, Mistress will personally supervise Paula's portions to ensure she does lose weight as planned.

As it was to be a very special occasion Paula was also allowed to choose a small amount of jewellery. She chose a long a long purple beaded neckless and some long, thin earrings to set the neckless off.

Paula herself was slowly becoming excited about the big night ahead and forgetting the competition element of the evening, which

Mistress and the other dominants were adding the finishing touches to add excitement and intrigue to the proceedings. Paula was the only submissive to know in advance that she will have to earn her collar on the night, for the others it is a surprise to come. Although there will also be some surprises for Paula too.

Mistress ordered for herself a long full-length black leather dress and knee-length red leather boots. She also ordered lots of new makeup products for herself and Paula. Lastly, she ordered a new black braided dressage whip which no doubt Paula would feel before the evening was out. This was to be a no expense spared evening and one for both of them to remember for a long time into the future. It was a public demonstration of the level of commitment and that Mistress Anastasia and Paula were devoted to each other.

During the course of the next couple of weeks, there were to be some high-level meetings in Mistress Anastasia's house to finalise the course of events for the collaring ceremonies. No submissives were allowed into these meetings and the submissives, sissies, and slaves, including Paula, congregated in the kitchen until their Masters and Mistresses come out of the living room at the end of their conference.

This was a mini holiday for Paula as normally she would have to serve during such get-togethers, but on these special evenings, the dominants had to serve themselves to preserve the secrecy. No sub was to know in advance what he or she was in for on the night.

Chapter Eight.

Getting ready for the big night.

The talk was of nothing else in the last week before the collaring. Paula was excused from normal duties so she could help her Mistress with the preparations. There was much to be done. One of Paula's jobs was to print and envelope the invitations and take them to the mailbox at the end of the street.

Mistress Anastasia was to be the Officiant and leader of the ceremonies. It was her job to keep order and make the whole collaring process to be as entertaining as possible. Being a confident extrovert, she relished the opportunity to prove her hosting skills.

It was decided she would also conduct each collaring except for her own. She had chosen, the owner of the club a Master himself to preside over Paula's collaring. She particularly wanted this Master because he looked the part and had a very commanding voice.

Mistress had spent nearly an entire week on her laptop writing a script for each individual collaring at the request of their Masters and Mistresses. She would also say a word or two of encouragement for those who failed the test and would forfeit the collaring that night.

It was up to each couple to write any vows they may want at the ceremony and we had to write ours of course, which was a cross between a speech and several quotes pinched from the Internet. Mistress Anastasia drew up a contract which we would both sign on the night committing Paula to a lifetime of drudgery and service. The contract laid out what she can and cannot do and what is permissible to wear in service and out.

Paula concluded there was more to a collaring than a conventional wedding. Especially as all the submissives had to perform tests to demonstrate their worthiness to be collared by their respective Mistresses and Masters. Mistress Anastasia didn't believe this had ever been done before and might start a new trend for future collarings.

On the evening of the collaring Mistress Anastasia and Paula spent hours getting ready. Paula's makeup had to be perfect. Paula had to present herself to her Mistress to be checked over and was sent back to the bedroom several times to redo her makeup. They would change into their special costumes after they arrived at the club.

Each time Paula dressed and presented herself to her mistress, she was sent away to try better. Paula felt the riding crop on her buttocks more than once, as Mistress was becoming quite stressed and would take her frustrations out on poor Paula's backside. Dressed and ready both Mistress and maid drenched themselves in perfume, Anastasia ordered a taxi and waited in the hall for it to come as it was raining cats and dogs outside.

"I hope this awful weather doesn't affect the attendance tonight," Mistress said, getting all fretful and worried "We might be the only ones there, that would be a disaster, especially after spending so much money on hiring the club for the night."

We intentionally arrived very early to make last-minute adjustments and tweaks on the site. Anastasia and Paula were the first ones there, but that was what Mistress planned and wasn't too worried at this point that they were on their own. Mistress was relieved when finally guests began to arrive in trickles and drabs.

On arrival, there were drinks and snacks provided in the foyer in the form of a buffet. It was an opportunity for guests to mingle before the events of the evening began in earnest. Mistress Anastasia had put a temporary collar and lead on Paula, so everywhere Mistress went Paula was forced to follow. Paula had a job to keep up as Mistress had she had quite a stride and poor Paula was wearing new three-inch heels and it wasn't long before Paula felt blisters emerging on her toes as she hobbled along to catch her Mistress up.

"It's a good turnout," Mistress shouted to Paula over the din of music and chatter. "I have done a quick headcount and as far as I can tell everyone has shown up despite the storm outside. I am so happy and pleased tonight is going to be a big success."

Having done the rounds and chatted to everyone that mattered, Mistress Anastasia poured herself and Paula a drink and decided to find a table to rest their feet for a little while, it was to be a long night, and they needed to pace themselves.

"Normally, you would sit on the floor Paula like a good slave should, but I don't want you spoiling your dress for later, so you may sit on a seat tonight." Paula sat down to great relief as her feet were stinging from chaffed blisters, but no sooner she sat Mistress ordered her to her feet again.

"That is not how a lady sits Paula," Mistress admonished, stand up and sit again the way I taught you. Remember Paula you're on your best behaviour tonight, don't you dare go letting me down."

"No Mistress," Paula replied, sitting down more gracefully and in the prescribed manner.

"That's better Paula, think deportment, or you will suffer later when I get you home. You haven't seen me yet when I am really annoyed."

Mistress Anastasia sipped her drink and did a mental headcount and when she was fairly sure all the couples for the collaring ceremony had arrived. She stood and clapped her hands loudly to get everyone's attention. In seconds the dim of chatter had transformed into silence as the audience awaited Mistress Anastasia's next utterance.

"I am glad you could all make it here through the storm this evening to witness the grand collaring ceremony." Mistress paused for a second and added. "I will be an evening to remember. Now you have all had a drink and something to snack on let us all go into the grand hall. " Mistress Anastasia said, pointing to a double door to her right. As she spoke the doors were opened by two smartly dressed maids and everyone took their drinks and headed inside.

Chapter Nine

The Tasks.

Mistress Anastasia and Paula following on her leash made their way through the throng of people and up onto the stage. Paula was allowed to wait backstage while her Mistress went forward to the edge of the stage to address the crowd.

"Attention, attention everybody. This is a special night for us all. We all know how important collaring is, and the degree of effort both Master and slave put into their shared commitment. Because a collaring is so important tonight before the collaring ceremonies begin all the submissives to be collared must prove to their Master and Mistress's they are worthy of the collar they are about to receive.

So with all the Masters and Mistress's permission, we have set a series of tasks for each submissive to perform and only those that pass all the tests will be collared tonight. The remaining submissives will have to go back to their owners for more intensive training and be collared on another night."

The audience clapped with approval and when the applause died down Mistress Anastasia continued:

"Each submissive must perform several separate tasks, all the tasks will be the same for each candidate. The tasks will be performed here on the stage for all to see. When the competition begins each Master and Mistress will bring their submissive up onto the stage to be introduced before the first task begins. To start the task off, let me introduce my submissive and sissy maid Paula." Mistress Anastasia beckoned Paula to come forward from behind the curtains and make herself known to the audience.

Paula gingerly stepped forward and stood before her Mistress and gave a nervous but respectful curtsey to the audience.

"Paula," Mistress bellowed for effect, "stand here and take your panties off. All the other contestants, please come onto the stage and stand at Paula's side in a row. You may too take off your pants and panties."

Everyone obeyed and took off their underpants and put them on the ground in front of them. There were twenty contestants in total, including Paula and they filled the width of the stage. At Mistress Anastasia's command, they all spread their legs in unison as if on a parade ground. As all the contestants were male it made the next task easier, as their respective Masters and Mistresses attached a parachute to the testicles of each contestant.

"Attention everyone," Mistress Anastasia urged as the room filled with chatter again. " Each contestant will have one of these fishing weights dropped into the parachute every minute. Each weight weighs an ounce If the pain gets too much the contestant may retire, but the first to go will retire from the competition and forfeit the collaring. Let the show begin," Mistress Anastasia said, dropping the first weight into Paula's parachute. Mistress kissed Paula on the cheek and whispered:

"Don't you dare go and let me down, Paula?"

The minutes passed and the line of submissives began to look untidy as they swayed back and forth to try and dissipate the pain. After six minutes the first contestants began to drop out at the disgust and annoyance of their owners. Nine minutes in total had passed before the required entrants dropped out of the completion. As soon as the losers were identified the parachutes were taken off the remaining contestants to gasps of relief.

Paula in particular couldn't wait for this test to end as she was at the end of her tether and was moments away from throwing the towel in. Just one more weight and she would have been forced to capitulate. Her poor testicles throbbed long after the parachute was removed. However, she realised this was only the beginning and there were many tasks to go before she would qualify to be collared.

The contestants for the second task had to remain on the stage, but were allowed to sit on the floor whilst preparations were made for their next ordeal. Mistress Anastasis went off stage and back into the audience to mingle and sip her drink before returning on stage for the next test. Paula sat on the stage with the others and nursed her sore testicles.

While Mistress was mingling, several hard-backed chairs were brought onto the stage and placed in front of each entrant, who was then ordered to stand up and await instructions.

"Attention contestants," Mistress Anastasia bellowed as she clambered back onto the stage. She was enjoying the power she had over the unwitting souls. "All of you stand on your chairs and put your arms out to your side." Mistress puts her arms out to demonstrate what she wanted them to do. "The first to drop their arms are out of the contest, leaving the remainder for the next round. Trust me, slaves, the tasks will get more difficult as we progress. This is just an easy one to get you all in the mood."

With a clap of Mistress's hands, all the entrants climbed on the chair and held their arms out at their sides as shown and instructed. Paula smiled to herself as she was well-versed in this particular torture and was fairly confident that she would not be the first to succumb. Within a few moments, some of the contestants were already beginning to crumble. The audience showed their displeasure when after only three minutes one of the contestants dropped his arms to his side. A very angry Master came onto the stage and removed the offending submissive with the end of his riding crop. Not many would want to be in that submissive's shoes for the remainder of the evening and beyond.

Next, the remaining lucky contestants had to stand in a line, one behind the other. Mistress Anastasia showed the audience a thick light pink leather tawse. It was approximately eighteen inches long and around an eighth of an inch thick. The colour pink was very deceptive as this was a true implement of torture, The tawse had a very little bend in it as Mistress held it up to show the audience. Then Anastasia went on to give a potted history of this Scottish implement of chastisement. The punishment would be administered to the hapless contestants, in the time-honoured fashion on the hands.

Paula once again was the first submissive to endure the punishment and had to step forward from the queue and put her hands out flat palms up in front of her. Mistress Anastasia rested the tawse gently on Paula's hand, almost tickling it, then she raised it and brought it down with a deafening thud. Paula reeled in pain as her hand throbbed from the impact.

"Now the other hand," Mistress urged, hardly giving Paula time enough to get over the pain of the first stroke. Paula crossed her hands over and the second stroke hurt even more until a full five strokes on each hand were administered. Paula was close to tears at the end of this punishment.

Paula stepped aside to nurse her poor throbbing hands while the next in line stepped forward for the same treatment from their respective Master or Mistress. This punishment went on for ages until one contestant broke down in tears and retired from the contest, which was a relief to Paula, who dreaded the second round of ten strokes from the tawse. However, it made her wonder what the remaining entrants had to endure next.

There was another pause in the proceeding to give the contestants a bit of a break and to allow their owners to return to the tables for a drink, while others went outside into the cold night air to take advantage of a break in the rain for a smoke. However, the break was short as there was a long night ahead and still several contestants to eliminate before the actual collaring ceremonies could begin.

Eager to get on with the proceedings Mistress Anastasia returned to the stage and clapped rigorously to get everyone's attention.

"There are still contestants to eliminate so we need to get on with the show," Anastasia said in a bellowing voice. "The next round is twelve strokes of the riding crop on the bare bottom. If none drops out, the twelve strokes will be repeated until someone throws the towel in. As usual, my slave Paula will be first on the spanking bench."

As Mistress Anastasis spoke a spanking bench was brought onto the stage and placed in the centre so all in the audience could see the action. Paula stepped forward and bent over the contraption and three willing slaves tied her down so she couldn't move an inch. With several flicks of a crop Mistress, Anastasia began the punishment. To be fair to the other contestants and to show no favouritism, she brought down the crop hard on Paula's bottom. Almost immediately the freshly laid white stroke marks turned to a swollen, angry red and some of Paula's pimples started to bleed. Paula winced and struggled in her restraints. However, with tears in her eyes, she managed to survive all twelve strokes of the crop. Much to Paula's regret, everyone survived the first twelve strokes, and Paula was once again over the spanking bench for the second batch of twelve strokes of the riding crop.

Paula's bottom stung and throbbed as each of the strokes was delivered on an already very sore bottom often striking where she had been struck on the previous round. If she was at home Paula would have begged Mistress Anastasia to stop and may have used her safe word, but here with a large audience, Paula couldn't face the humiliation of throwing the towel in and survived all twelve strokes. When she was released from the spanking bench Mistress Anastasia brushed Paula's tears away with her fingers and kissed the hapless girl on the cheeks and told Paula how well she had done, and her Mistress was proud of her.

As it transpired Paula was very unlucky as she was the only submissive to get twenty-four strokes and the submissive next to go on the spanking bench, threw in the towel almost immediately after only the first two strokes of the second batch were administered.

Now there were fewer contests left to eliminate before the collaring could begin and the stage was set for the next endurance test.

This time several low benches were brought onto the stage and set next to each other head to toe making a long line of benches. All the remaining contestants were told to lie on the ground on their backs and place their legs over the bench to expose their bare feet. The audience muttered and whispered to one another, knowing this punishment will be excruciatingly painful for the remaining contestants. No one would want to swap places with the hapless contestants on the stage tonight.

Mistress Anastasia selected a thick, sturdy cane and swished it several times, and smirked approval before going to the end of the benches, where you have probably guessed poor Paula was the first in the line. Without further word Mistress Anastasia brought the cane down hard on the soles of each of Paula's bare feet. Paula let out an almighty scream of agony.

Before Paula barely recovered Mistress Anastasia was halfway down the line of benches having administered a single stroke to each of the contestant's feet. Fortunately, there was no second round as the pain from these strokes caused a hapless contestant to give up after only one foot was caned. There was so much screaming and agony that the audience was not surprised one fell by the wayside so soon, and even the contestant's Mistress didn't admonish the poor submissive too much for dropping out of the competition so quickly.

The number of contestants was, dropping and there were only a few to eliminate from the competition. Mistress Anastasia was anxious to get the collaring started and decided to make the endurance tests harder for the remaining contestants to speed up the dropout rate.

The next test was about to begin and each contestant had to stand in a line facing forward with their legs wide open, revealing their genitalia for all the audience to see. Mistress

Anastasia as usual began by addressing the audience:

"On this test, she announced the victims will be whipped on their penis with the flap of the riding crop until they beg to stop. My assistant," Mistress said, pointing to a young girl at her side, " will time how long it takes for the submissive to last before begging to stop. The contestant with the shortest time leaves the competition. Let's get started, Mistress Anastasia shouted to the audience with enormous enthusiasm as she whisked her riding crop through the air, making a sound, that will make any submissive wince.

Once again Paula was the first to get the treatment. Mistress Anastasia told Paula to stand with her legs open as wide as possible, then Mistress began to whip her penis while the assistant started the stopwatch. Finally, Paula wriggled in pain and begged Mistress Anastasia to stop. Despite the begging, Mistress landed another two strokes before she finished.

The assistant stopped the watch, before the extra strokes and said Paula had lasted an impressive five minutes and 59 seconds. Poor Paula's little penis was throbbing and very sore, but she knew she had survived to the next round as the shortest time recorded was just over three minutes.

Now there were only a couple of contests to eliminate but time was marching on and the endurance tests were taking too long, so a group of Masters and Mistresses led by Mistress Anastasia huddled in a gaggle on stage and it was decided that the next test would be the final test and the last two contestants will drop out of the completion allowing the collaring ceremonies, the main event of the evening to begin.

It was only left for the impromptu group to decide what the last endurance test will be, it had to be something exceptional and spectacular to eliminate two contestants in one go.

The contestants were allowed off the stage to have a drink and some refreshments before being summoned back to the stage for the last endurance test. Mistress Anastasia stood in front of the contestants looking flushed and excited as she held up the microphone and announced:

"This is it, ladies and gentlemen, the last test of the evening before we start the collaring ceremonies. Each contestant will have to balance a book on their head whilst I go to each entrant and whip their backside once with a dressage whip. All the books will be the same size and weight for fairness. I will go up and down the row of contestants slowly whipping until the first two books fall. Needless to say, the first two to lose their books will be eliminated from the contest and will not be collared tonight."

Mistress Anastasia walked up to Paula the first in the row and whispered. "You had better pass this one my dear, or you'll be for it when we get home." Then she stood back three feet and cracked the long whip until the thin stingy end landed squarely on Paula's bottom. Paula let out an agonising scream and the book wobbled but by moving her body here and there she managed to stop it from toppling. This had Mistress worried for a second or two and sighed in relief when Paula managed to regain balance and keep the book from falling.

Paula was extremely lucky to have survived that round as the next two in a row dropped their books bringing a quick conclusion to the contest. They now had their winners and the collaring ceremonies can begin.

Chapter Ten

Let the ceremonies begin.

Finally the culmination of the whole evening the collaring ceremonies are about to begin. Mistress Anastasia and Paula were to be the last. The ceremonies began with a succession of Masters, Mistresses and their slaves coming onto the stage and giving their vows and pledges, each ceremony concluded with a roar of applause, and the collared couple, on leaving the stage would be given a box of chocolates and a complimentary glass of bubbly each to enjoy all paid for by Mistress Anastasia. The failed contestants could only watch and wish it will be their turn next time.

Mistress Anastasia decided to give poor Paula a bit of a break, she was allowed to sit at the table and was even waited on with a drink so she could relax and prepare mentally for her big advent. Although time was marching on it only seemed fair to give Paula a little bit of downtime.

Then after a short rest, both Mistress Anastasia and Paula went off to the changing rooms to change into their collaring costumes. Mistress struggled to get into her tight-fitting black leather dress. Puffed out and exhausted Mistress Anastasia sat down on a stool to recover from sliding into a dress that was probably one size too small. Too late now, nevertheless, she looked commanding and the dress and red leather boots gave her great presence and were a perfect choice to demonstrate her powerful presence and dominant nature.

Paula also put on her dress which is in direct contrast to her Mistress's. Paula's dress is a soft fabric white midi dress with subtle puffed shoulders. Around her waist is a purple belt of the same fabric tied into a neat bow at the side of her waist. All set off with cream 3-inch stilettos and earrings and neckless. Paula in contrast projected a picture of sissy beauty and submissiveness. They both admired themselves in a mirror and remarked on how stunning they looked and left the changing rooms to return to the stage and bar.

When the crowd saw Mistress Anastasia and Paula emerge from the changing rooms everyone applauded and whistled their approval. A sissy maid came over and gave Mistress and Paula a glass of bubbly. After a short chat with their admirers, they finished sipping their drinks and walked up onto the stage. Once on the stage, the applause restarted and by this time was much louder than before. Mistress Anastasia guided Paula to the middle and centre of the stage. The clapping and applauding went on for ages and when it eventually died down Mistress said to Paula.

"On your knees." Paula submissively and daintily sank to her knees and bowed her head. In the meantime, another sissy maid rushed over with a low table with Paula's new collar in the centre and a metal rod with a capital letter 'A' welded to the end along with Mistress's new braided dressage whip. The table was placed between Mistress and Paula. Paula out of the corner of her eye glanced over at the table and began to panic when she saw the metal rod next to her new collar and realised it was a branding iron.

The most senior Master and owner of the club came onto the stage and hushed the audience.

He was a tall, plump fellow with a full white beard and a commanding voice.

"It is with my great pleasure," he bellowed, "to officiate and collar Mistress Anastasia's slave Paula. Whilst the host was talking, two slaves brought a metal drum onto the stage. One slave poured in coke and firelighters and the other slave using a lighter set it ablaze. Flames quickly roared into the air and the audience became excited at such a sight, wondering what it was all for.

"Mistress Anastasia," shouted the host," Will you please put the branding iron on the stove to heat it up ready for use later". Now a spanking bench was brought onto the stage. "Paula," demanded the host, "please come and bend over the spanking bench."

Paula did as she was told and whilst she was being tied down by slaves, Mistress picked up the dressage whip and flicked it through the air which made a very impressive snapping and whistling sound.

Mistress turned to speak to the audience and announced. "Paula will receive fifty strokes of the whip as an introduction to a lifetime as my slave. Paula knew the dressage whip would be used, as Mistress would not have purchased it for the occasion, but she had no idea she was to receive fifty strokes as a part of the collaring ceremony. There seemed to be quite a few things about the ceremony Paula wasn't told, hence all the secret meetings at the house.

Mistress Anastasia stepped forward and began to expertly lay the whip on poor Paula's buttocks. It was quite a visual thing to see this long, thin whip flying through the air several feet to land squarely on Paula's buttocks. Paula's buttocks quivered like blancmange as each stroke landed. This was very visual for the audience and there was silence whilst the punishment was administered.

Almost immediately white lines appeared where the whip had landed, quickly followed by more turning to an angry red. Soon Paula's whole bottom was covered in red angry and swollen whip strokes, including her thighs and upper legs. After about twenty strokes Paula began to cry and strain against her bonds.

Eventually, to a silenced audience, the fifty strokes were concluded. Paula was a sobbing heap at this stage. Slaves rushed forward to untie Paula from the spanking bench.

"Paula come back to the table, please," the host barked. "Stand facing your Mistress," the man said, turning Paula with his hands on her waist as if she hadn't heard his instructions. Mistress Anastasia smiled at Paula and picked up her new collar and held it with both hands close to her chest as the host continued to speak.

"Paula, do promise to serve your Mistress, selflessly and diligently for the rest of your life?" The man paused for Paula's reply.

"I do," said Paula, fighting back a dry throat. As she spoke two slaves wheeled an A-frame onto the stage and parked it behind Mistress, Paula, and the host.

"You'll see on the stove at your side a branding iron with your Mistress's initial 'A' ". The man picked up the branding iron which glowed bright red for Paula to see. Paula could feel the heat coming off the iron, despite it being a few feet away.

"Do you accept the brand?" This was the first Paula knew of the intended branding, Mistress Anastasia had said nothing about branding, just there was to be a big surprise for her, which she wasn't joking this was one hell of a surprise, which had put Paula off guard as she hadn't expected it or imagined such a thing in her wildest dreams.

Paula wasn't the slightest bit happy about being branded, a tattoo perhaps, but a real branding was going to hurt as nothing has hurt before. It was also going to be extremely painful long after the event and for weeks and weeks to come. Yet despite all this Paula felt intimidated by his Mistress's gaze and the expectant audience. How could she refuse now? The subsequent humiliation and embarrassment would be harder to endure than the branding itself.

"I accept the brand," Paula said hardly believing her own words. A slave stepped forward and picked up the branding iron from the stove and on the host's instructions plunged it back deep into the glowing coals. Another slave rushed forward with a clipboard and passed it to the host.

"Mistress Anastasia," the host bellowed, so he could be heard across the floor and over the chatter of the audience. When silence resumed he continued. "Do you promise to own this slave for the rest of your life, discipline her and encourage her to become a better slave?"

"I do," Mistress Anastasia said, brushing away an emotional tear from her face.

"I have before me, Paula a lifetime contract which your Mistress has drafted outlining your duties and commitments as Mistress's slave. Can you confirm you have read this document, approve and understand its contents before coming on the stage?"

"Yes," Paula replied.

"Sign here," the host insisted passing the clipboard over to Paula. She quickly signed it and passed it back to the man.

"That leaves two things left to do," the host said addressing the audience. "Mistress Anastasia will you put the collar on Paula Mistress stepped closer to Paula kissed her on the forehead and attached the purple collar which looked like a treat. Yet again the audience burst into applause.

"You are to wear your collar day and night," Mistress said to Paula loudly so the audience could hear. Now I shall lock it in place. " Mistress Anastasia concluded, putting on the little heart-shaped lock and snapping it into place. The key was on a fine chain Mistress put around her neck as a symbolic gesture of the commitment they were both entering into.

"Now that leaves what we were all waiting for, the branding. Is the iron hot enough?" The officiant shouted to the slave tending the stove. The slave held up the iron which was glowing bright orange.

"Yes Sir," the slave replied. "The iron is now hot enough to be used."

"Paula step over to the 'A-frame and bend over." The man asked pointing to the frame. Paula did as she was told and two nearby slaves strapped her tightly to the frame. Then suspenseful music began to play in the background to add effect.

Mistress Anastasia stepped over and pulled up Paula's skirt and at the same time pulled down her panties.

"The branding iron will be administered by Mistress Anastasia herself and the brand will be placed on Paula's right buttock." The host said, pausing for effect and stepping out of the way so all could see what would happen next. He certainly had the attention of the audience as there was perfect silence, so much, if it wasn't for the music one could have heard a pin drop.

"Mistress Anastasia will you please pick up the branding iron and place it firmly on Paula's right buttock and hold it there for two whole seconds. Mistress picked up the branding iron and stepped over to Paula.

"I hereby brand my slave,' and almost before the words had finished being spoken down came the branding iron. The audience loudly counted one, two and Mistress Anastasia lifted the iron away from Paula's tortured buttocks. Meanwhile, Paula lurched and screamed as the smell of burning flesh filled the air.

Then Paula slumped into a semi-state of unconsciousness. The audience applauded and clapped and before Paula was freed from the frame members of the audience were allowed onto the stage to see the brand for themselves. The printed A on Paula's buttock cheek was big, red, and extremely angry. One, by one, the audience filled past the spectacle, giving admiring glances. Some stopped to tell Paula what a lucky girl she was to be honoured in such a way.

Paula was given a couple of weeks of light duties at home and recovered quickly. After a month the wound had healed up and the letter 'A' was clear for her Mistress to admire whenever she had the desire to whip or inspect her property.

The End

Check out my other books:

The Chronicles of a Male Slave.

A real-life account of a consensual slave. The book follows the life of an individual who comes to terms with his submissive side and his search for a Mistress and his subsequent experiences as a consensual slave.

This book gives a real insight into the B.D.S.M., lifestyle and what it is like to bc a real slave to a lifestyle Mistress.

Mistress Margaret.

This is the story of young teenage Brenden, who is finding out about his sexuality when he meets older Mistress Margaret a nonprofessional dominatrix. Mistress Margaret takes Brenden's hand and shows him the mysterious, erotic world of BDSM and all it has to offer.

The Week That Changed My Life.

A tale about a young girl discovering her sexuality with an older, more mature dominant man whilst on a week's holiday by the sea. She was introduced into a world of BDSM that would change her outlook on life forever.

The Temple of Gor.

Hidden in the wilds of Scotland is The Temple of Gor, a secret BDSM society. In the Temple you will find Masters and their female slaves living in a shared commune. The community is based on the Gorean subculture depicted in a fictional novel by John Norman and has taken a step too far and turned into a macabre reality. Stella a young girl from England, stumbles on the commune and is captured and turned into a Kajira slave girl until she finds a way to escape her captors.

Becoming a Sissy Maid.

This is a true story of one person's quest to become a sissy maid for a dominant couple. The story outlines the correspondence between the

Master, Mistress, and sissy maid, that lead up to their first and second real-time meeting.

It is a fascinating tale and is a true, honest and accurate account, only the names and places have been changed to protect the individuals involved. It is a must-be-read book by anyone into BDSM and will give an interesting insight for anyone wishing to become in the future a real-time sissy maid.

Meet Maisy The Sissy Maid.

This story is about Maisy a sissy maid and her life. The story takes Maisy through all the various stages a sissy has to make take to find her true submissive and feminine self. It is a long and arduous road and many transitions before Maisy finds true happiness as a lady's maid for her Mistress.

Beginner's Guide For The Serious Sissy

So you want to be a woman and dress and behave like a sissy? You accept you cannot compete with most men and now want to try something new and different. This guide will help you along the way and walk the potential sissy through the advantages and pitfalls of living as a submissive woman.

Becoming a serious sissy requires making changes that are both physical and mental. This will involve learning to cross-dress, leg-crossing, sit, stand, bend, do hair removal, wear makeup, use cosmetics, and sit down to pee. You'll learn feminine mannerisms such as stepping daintily, arching your spine, swishing your hips, and adopting a feminine voice. You'll understand more about hormone treatment and herbal supplements.

There is advice and tips on going out in public

for the first time and coming out of the closet to friends, colleagues, and family. The guide will give help you to slowly lose your masculine identity and replace it with a softer gentle feminine one.

The Secret Society.

Rene Glock is a freelance journalist looking for a national scoop and attempts to uncover and expose a Secret Society of Goreans which have set up residence in an old nightclub. However, as he delves into the secret world he finds he has an interest in BDSM and questions his moral right to interfere in what goes on in the Gorean Lodge.

The Good Master and Mistress Guide.

If you want to become a good Dominant and practice BDSM in a safe and considerate way, then this guide is for you.

It is written by a submissive that has had many dominants male and female over the years and knows what goes into becoming a good dominant and the mistakes some dominants make.

The book is not aimed to teach, but to make the fledgling dominant understand what is going on in the dominant-submissive dynamic, so they can understand their charges better and become better dominants.

My Transgender Journey

This is a true story with some minor alterations to protect people's identities. It is a tale about my own journey into transgender and my eventual decision to come out.

It is hoped that others can share my experiences, relate to them and perhaps take comfort from some of them.

The book has some BDSM content, but is only used to put my story into context, it's about my experiences, trials and tribulations of coming out and living as a female full-time.

I hope you enjoy my little story.

Cinders

Cinders is the BDSM version of Cinderella. It is a story where an orphaned Tommy is sent to be brought up by his aunt and two very beautiful sisters.

The sisters were cruel and taunting and dressed Tommy up like a Barbie Doll. One day Tommy was caught with auntie's bra and knickers and as a punishment, he was a feminist and turned into Nancy the maid. Poor Nancy is consigned to a life of drudgery and final acceptance of life as a menial skivvy.

This story doesn't have a glass slipper or a prince, but Nancy is given a present of some new rubber gloves and a bottle of bleach. There is no happy ending or is there, you decide.

At The Races

Ryan is a hotel night porter and is at a crossroads in his life. He feels his talents are being wasted in a job with no future. Through a friend, he is offered a managerial position on a farm in Catalonia, Spain. He decides to take the post, but has no idea what sort of farm he is going to work at.

Only on the flight out to Spain does Ryan realise that there is more to the farm than rearing chickens and growing vegetables. Later he learns the main event of the year is The Derby and there isn't a horse in sight.

I Nearly Married A Dominatrix

This is a true story that I have changed a little bit to protect people from identification. It's a story about a man's constant struggle and fights against his deep-rooted need to be submissive and a woman who conversely, is very comfortable with her dominance and heavily into the BDSM lifestyle.

They meet and get along very well indeed until Mistress Fiona announces she wants to become a professional dominatrix. Rex, the submissive boyfriend goes along with his Mistress's plans, reluctantly, but as time goes by there are more and more complications heaped on the relationship until it snaps.

Be careful what you ask for

There is an old English adage: Be careful about what you ask for; it may come true.

This is a story about a BDSM fantasy that has gone badly wrong.

Fantasy is simply a fantasy and we all have them regardless of our sexuality. Fantasies are quite harmless until we choose to act them out for real and when do act out our fantasies the line between fantasy and reality can become very blurred. This is a tale about one person's fantasy that becomes all too real for comfort.

Petticoat Lane.

A slightly effeminate young boy is taken under the wings of his school teacher. She becomes his guardian and trains him to become a servant girl to serve her for the rest of his life.

An unexpected incident happens and Lucy the maid has an opportunity to escape her life of drudgery and servitude, but does she take the opportunity or does she stay with her Mistress?

The Life and Times of a Victorian Maid.

This is a story about the life and times of a young Transgender who becomes a Victorian-style maid in a large exclusively B.D.S.M. household. Although fiction this story is largely based on fact, as the author herself lived in such a household for a while as a maid.

It shows the contrast between a place of safety where like-minded people can live in relative harmony and the need for ridged discipline in its serving staff.

There are many thriving households, such as the one mentioned here, tucked away out of sight and away from prying minds.

I Became a Kajira slave girl.

A Gorean scout Simon, who is looking for new talent kidnaps Emma a PhD student on sabbatical with her friend Zoey in Spain. Emma is half-drugged and sent across the ocean to the United States and ends up in the clandestine

City of Gor in the Mojave desert sixty miles from civilization.

Here there is no law women are mere objects for the pleasure of men. Emma becomes a Kajira a female slave whose sole purpose in life is to please her master or be beaten tortured or killed.

Two years into Emma's servitude and she meets Simon again. Simon is consumed with guilt when he sees what Emma has been reduced to, a beaten, downtrodden and abused slave. He vows to free her from her servitude, But how they are in one of the biggest deserts in the world and sixty miles from anywhere?

Training My First Sissy Maid.

A young single mother with a part-time job, two teenage children, and up to her knees in housework is at the end of her tether and finding it harder and harder to cope.

Then reading one of her daughter's kinky magazines she found in her bedroom whilst tidying, read an article about sissy maids who are willing to work without pay just for discipline, control and structure to their lives. Excited about the prospect she decides a maid is an answer to her domestic problems.

She sets about finding a sissy to come and do her housework and be trained and moulded into becoming her loyal obedient sissy maid. On the journey she discovers she is a natural dominant and training her maid becomes a highly erotic and fulfilling experience.

A Week with Mistress Sadistic.

Susan a young female reporter in her thirties wants to know more about B.D.S.M for a future article in her magazine. She arranged to spend a week with Mistress Sadistic and watch how a professional dominatrix works.

After an eye-opening week of watching Mistress Sadistic deal with her many and varied clients, Mistress Sadistic wonders if Susan might be submissive and puts her to the text to make Susan her personal slave.

Lady Frobisher and her maid Alice.

This is a gripping tale of BDSM in Victorian England. It is a story about the lives of Lady Frobisher and her hapless maid Alice. It is a tale of lesbianism and sexual sadism with a twist at the end.

If you enjoy reading BDSM literature you'll love this as it has everything woven into an interesting tale of two people's lives at the top end of society.

K9

This is a tale that explores an area of B.D.S.M where a Mistress or Master desires a human dog (submissive) to train and treat as a real dog in every respect. Mistress Cruella is one such Mistress who takes on a young male submissive as her human dog and she takes the role of Mistress and her dog very seriously indeed.

Ryan soon becomes Max the Poodle and he struggles with his new role as a pooch but learns to be an obedient dog to please his Mistress. Max soon discovers there is far more to being a dog than meets the eye.

Bridget Monroe's Finishing School for Sissies.

Bridget and her husband are both dominant and have their own sissy maid Isabel to help them with housework. One day when the couple were on holiday in Kent, Bridget discovered an empty manor house in need of extensive repairs. On inquires, she decides to buy the manor but soon realises that to pay for the mortgage and repair costs the manor house will need to be run as a business.

Bridget used willing slaves in the B.D.S.M., community to help repair and renovate the manor house and later it was decided on advice from friends to open the manor house as a finishing school for sissies. A business had been born and later other B.D.S.M., activities were added to the core business, which included torture rooms and a medieval dungeon. Once a month an open day was held at the academy held pony races, yard sales and schoolboy classes. This also included K9 dog shows, beer tents and other amenities intending to satisfy the whole B.D.S.M., community.

Just when the business was taking off and in profit disaster struck. Society wasn't ready for Bridget Monroe's Finishing School for Sissies and Bridget was forced to close.

.

Printed in Great Britain
by Amazon

38243086R10096